DARK CLAW

Tunnel Mazers

May the Guiding Paw be with you!

Hodder
Children's
Books

First published in Great Britain in 2002
by Hodder Children's Books

10 9 8 7 6 5 4

A Catalogue record for this book is available from the
British Library

ISBN 0 340 81754 2

Printed and bound in Great Britain by
Bookmarque Ltd, Croydon, Surrey

Hodder Children's Books
a division of Hodder Headline Limited
338 Euston Road
London NW1 3BH

Chapter 1

"Now!" hissed Dark Claw.

The Dark Moon control room sprang to life.

Lights flashed. Screens lit up.
Somewhere on the secret space station
an awesome weapon prepared to fire.
Dark Claw smiled an evil smile.

Near by, a passing Muss spaceship
came under attack.

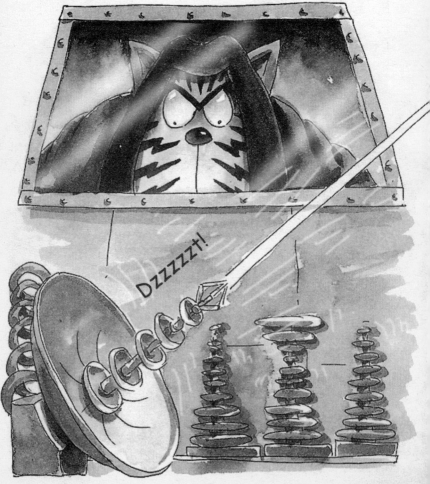

Dzzzzzt!

"Help! Our Nosar circuits have blown!" screamed the Muss Captain. "The ship is out of control-o-o-o-o-o-l!"

The small craft hurtled towards the Great Black Hole, and was never seen again.

Chapter 2

There is nothing in the known universe that stinks like Fworgonzola.

Dark Claw owned the biggest piece of Fworgonzola ever known. He had used it to build his deadly Stonker Ray.

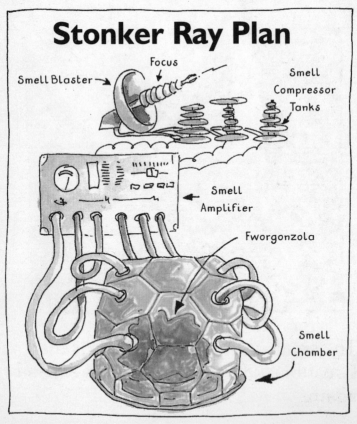

The Stonker Ray would destroy the Muss Nosar systems and cause chaos for Muss spaceships.

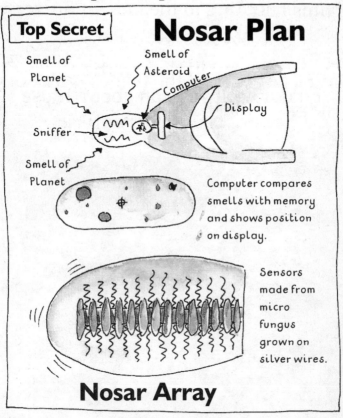

Without their Nosar, the Muss could not find their way through space. This was just the beginning of Dark Claw's master plan . . . to destroy the whole Muss race!

First he sent out a squadron of robot Seekahs to gather information on his enemy. (Kats like to play with their victims first!)

Chapter 3

One of the Seekahs flew across the Muss desert towards a strange building. It was the Tan Monastery School for gifted young Muss.

The Seekah hovered silently by a window and looked in. Inside, three young Muss were deep in conversation.

"I wish we could win the Tunnel Mazing Cup," said Hammee, the one with glasses. "The first prize is going to be a huge cheddar cheese."

Onlee One, the one with sticking-up hair, sighed. "If odely I was bord wid a sedse of sbell," he said. "Thed our teab bight win for a change."

"Never mind," said Chin Chee, the one with the hair band. "You can't be the best at *everything!*"

The Seekah flew off. But we shall stay with these three young ones.

Chapter 4

Later, at tunnel-mazing practice, the games teacher, Father Dug, gave his Muss pupils their instructions.

There are two ways out today. One exit has a Cheddar cheese smell and the other smells of Red Leicester. These smells are very similar. It'll be tricky, but good practice for the finals at the end of term. The first team to come out at the cheddar cheese hole wins.

Hammee squeaked,
"Can we eat it if we win, sir?"

Father Dug smiled.
Hammee was always hungry.

We'll see.

Thirty young Muss poured into the
dark tunnels. Sniffing like mad, they
searched for the cheesy smells that
would lead them to the right exit.

"Phwoor!" someone called out in the darkness. "I can smell Tansy's feet!"

Our trio made a good team. Chin Chee was an excellent smeller. Hammee could find food a hundred miles away, and Onlee One had a razor-sharp photographic memory.

Along the way, he drew a map of the tunnels in his head. If only he could smell as well, he'd be world champion.

Onlee One spotted the faint glow of
light from the exit.

They scrambled out of the hole, but Amber's team had beaten them. They were already outside.

Amber sniggered and waved the pieces of cheese. "Hey Hammee, look what we've got!"

Hammee was livid. "They always win. It's so unfair!" he complained.

Onlee One's keen eyes spotted
something in the far distance.

"What is that?!" he called out.
It was a while before the others saw
what he was pointing at.

A long, black car swept down the
desert road towards them.

"It bust be sub-wun really ib-portant," said Onlee One.

"Or someone really famous!" added Chin Chee.

The car cruised through the school gates and parked out of sight.

Who could it be?
They would have to wait to find out.

Chapter 5

They were just finishing supper that night, when the cook called out,

Onlee One,
The Abbot wants
to see you.

Onlee One's stomach lurched.
What could he have done wrong?
Everyone watched
and whispered
as he made his
way out of the
dining-room.

Good Luck!

The cook knocked on the door of Abbot Grey's study. Onlee One looked up at the name boards on the wall. They listed all the tunnel-mazing champions for over a hundred years. One name stood out in red paint.

The cook saw what he was looking at and sighed. "Pale One... He was the greatest champion of all."

School Champions

Pale One	Pale One
Pale One	Pale One
Pale One	Pale One
Pale One	Pale One
Valmeer	Calmor
	Vincent

Onlee One nodded. He had heard many stories about Pale One. There had never been a tunnel-mazer like him before or since.

The cook winked at him. "If you try hard enough, you could be like him one day."

Onlee One shrugged. "It's dot very likely. We bight share de saymb sir-naymb, but he didn't have by doze!"

Just then Abbot Grey opened his door.
He smiled when he saw Onlee One's
worried face.

Onlee One went inside and The Abbot closed the door behind him.

I'd like you to meet two of our old students. I taught them both when they were much younger.

Chapter 6

Onlee One gasped. He felt he knew the visitors already. Their pictures were in the papers every day. His stomach gurgled loudly as he was introduced to Top Muss, President of the Planet, and Brandling, the Chancellor!

"I-I-Ib pleased to beet you?" he stammered.

Abbot Grey told him to sit down.

Then Top Muss began to tell of the peril faced by every single Muss.

Our Planet is in great danger. We need a very special and brave young Muss to save us all from certain destruction. Onlee One, we think you are that Muss!

Top Muss told Onlee One about Dark Claw and the Stonker Ray. He showed him a tiny piece of Fworgonzola that was sealed in a glass tube.

Tiny amounts are used to flavour food. But the smell from just this little speck would blast our noses and leave us like you, unable to smell.

Brandling explained their plan.

Because you have no sense of smell, you'll be able to get close to the Stonker Ray and destroy it. We captured one of Dark Claw's Seekahs and adapted it to carry a small Muss inside.

That is how we plan to get you on Dark Moon. It is a very dangerous mission. The whole planet is relying on you.

Onlee One gulped. "Why does this Dark Claw want to destroy us all?"

Top Muss gave a deep sigh. "If only we knew."

Silence filled the room while Onlee One made up his mind. It was such a big challenge. Onlee One's legs shook just thinking about it. But, deep down, he was thrilled to have been chosen."

He took a deep breath.

I will serve you well, but odly if Hammee and Chin Chee cub with be. I need a teamb that I can trust.

Hammee and Chin Chee were sent for and agreed to join Onlee One on his mission.

"If Onlee One gets out alive, he'll need us to rescue him," said Chin Chee.

The Abbot nodded. "Any other questions?" he asked.

Hammee lifted a finger.

Any chance of extra food rations...

Chapter 7

The three young Muss were taken to a secret training camp. Chin Chee and Hammee spent hours each day, learning to fly a Whisker 320 Space Scout.

Woosh!

Chin Chee loved every minute.

Meanwhile, Hammee made sure there were plenty of food rations hidden around the spaceship... just in case!

Onlee One was taught to fly the captured Seekah. It was a tight squeeze, and hard to fly smoothly. It took a lot of practice.

Two weeks later, the three Muss were fully trained and their ship was ready to take Onlee One to Dark Moon.

Chapter 8

It was cold inside the Seekah.

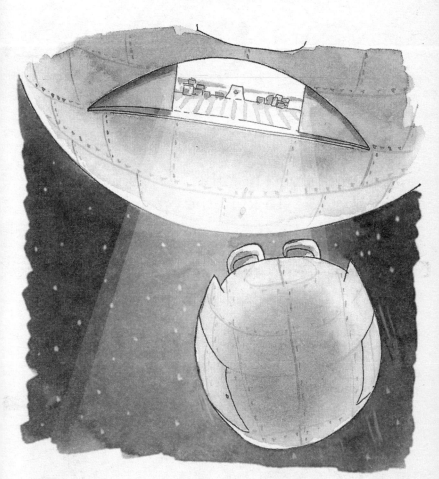

The air-lock doors opened and let Onlee One inside Dark Moon.

He landed the little craft in the
shadows, where he hoped no one
would see him open the hatch.

A door opened noisily.
A Robo Kat stood in the opening.
Onlee One froze.
Could it see him?

Another dumpy robot rumbled in.
The door closed behind it.
Onlee One had learned his lessons
well. The robot was a standard model:
RU12 Utility-Kat.

Remembering his training, Onlee One crept up behind it and pressed two red buttons on its back.

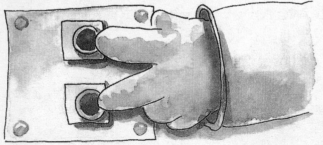

The robot froze.

Three seconds later, the robot clicked and switched off.

"It worked!" thought Onlee One. "They said by photographic bebbory would cub in handy!"

The hatch in the side of the robot opened easily, and Onlee One climbed through. He looked for the red and white wires.

He cut them,

stripped them

and reconnected them.

Now he could control the robot from the inside. He could move around Dark Moon without being noticed.

The door opened for him. The guard
turned and stared.

Onlee One heard his heart pounding,
but the guard didn't notice.
It stood to attention.

The door closed behind the young
Muss. He had passed the first test.

Chapter 9

Onlee One was having fun. The other robots didn't suspect a thing.

He pottered around the corridors, trying the doors to see what was behind them.

All the time he drew a map of Dark Moon in his head. If the mission was successful he'd know how to get back to his Seekah.

On Level Three he struck lucky. Two guards stood outside a door. The door opened. He went in and the door closed behind him.

A large machine stood in the middle of the room. It had to be the Stonker Ray.

Onlee One squeezed out of the
robot and took a closer look.
Yes, there in the middle of the
machine was a piece of Fworgonzola
the size of a ting-tong ball!

He studied the control panel.
One button said eject. He pushed it.
The Fworgonzola slid out on a tray.
Onlee One picked it up and sniffed.

"Oh! I thingk I cad sbell sum-ting!" he
said aloud.

As he spoke, the door swished open.
Onlee One spun round.
A tall, hooded figure stood before him.
Yellow eyes glowed with rage.

"GUARDS!" boomed Dark Claw.
"Seize him!"

Chapter 10

Robo Kats filled the room.

Onlee One looked for an escape.
The door was the only way out.
It was blocked.

There was only one thing for it:
EAT THE FWORGONZOLA!

He popped it into his mouth and
swallowed hard. Yuck!
It tasted like old shoe leather!

Dark Claw gasped, "I'll never find so much Fworgonzola again!"

The Robo Kats tried to grab Onlee One.

A bright light burst inside Onlee One's head. Then he sneezed so loud he could have turned himself inside out.

Choo!

The Robo Kats were confused.
They turned to Dark Claw for
instructions.

Onlee One sniffed.

Then he
sniffed again.

He laughed out loud.

I can smell!

The Robo Kats' paws couldn't hold him tight enough. He wriggled from their grasp and dived for the door, but not before Dark Claw lashed at him. Onlee One felt warm blood trickle down his arm.

He felt fearless! He ran and ran, somersaulting over Robo Kats. None of them could catch him.

The map in his head was clear as day. He came to the passage where the Robo Kat stood guard over the air-lock hangar door.

"Hey, Metal Boy, over here!" Onlee One taunted it.

The young Muss ran at the Robo Kat. He threw himself on the floor and slid right between its legs. He was through the door in no time.

Inside the hangar, he pressed the button to open the air-lock and squeezed inside the Seekah.

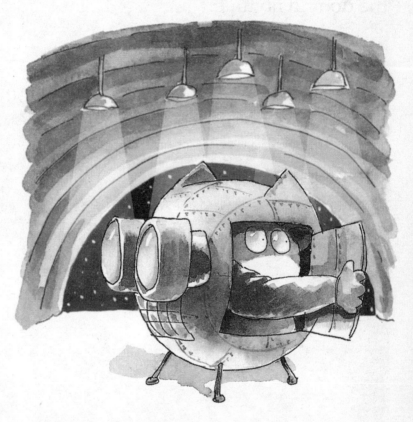

The Seekah's hatch sealed just in time. Dark Moon's air-lock doors opened and the vacuum of space sucked Onlee One out of the hangar bay, into the vast darkness.

He hit a switch to start the radio signal
his friends were waiting for.
In ten minutes, Chin Chee and
Hammee caught him in a net and
pulled him to the safety of their ship.

Chapter 11

A week later, Hammee and Chin Chee held the huge Cheddar cheese high above their heads and danced.

The annual school tunnel-mazing final had been a walkover. With Onlee One's fantastic new sense of smell, the trio smashed all school records!

Chancellor Brandling was the guest of honour. She leaned close and spoke quietly to Onlee One as she gave him his prize.

That's two remarkable performances, young one! I'm sorry we have to keep the first one a secret. Every living Muss owes you a great debt. If only they knew. I hope you feel this cup is a worthy consolation?

Onlee One took the cup from her.
It was a simple design, but it meant
more to him than Brandling could ever
imagine. The names of all the winners
were engraved on the side.

Onlee One was so proud.
He fought down the tears.

It's an honour to
follow in the footsteps of
great tunnel- mazers like
Pale One.

The crowd picked him up and carried him on their shoulders as they cheered and clapped their new Champion.

Brandling watched the scene from the edge of the crowd.

"I'm sure we will meet again, young One," she whispered to herself.

Chapter 12

Meanwhile, on Dark Moon,
Dark Claw raged.

"Revenge!" he howled.

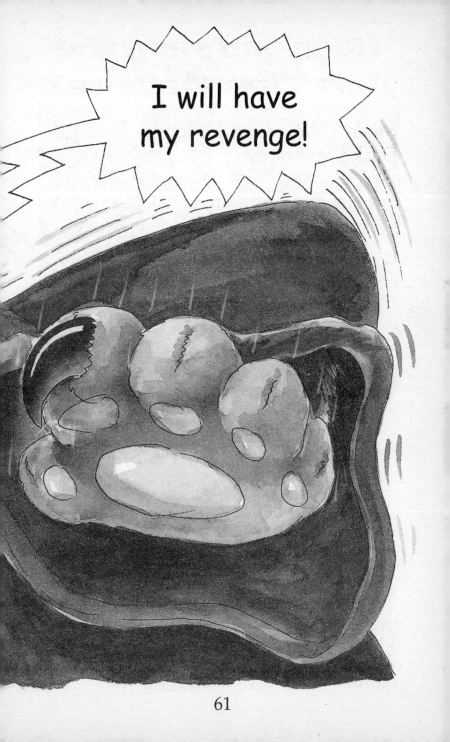